THE USBORNE YOUNG SCIENTIST
HUMAN BODY

Susan Meredith, Ann Goldman and Tom Lissauer
Designed by Roger Priddy

Contents

Illustrated by Kuo Kang Chen, Dee McLean, Sue Stitt, Penny Simon
and Rob McCaig

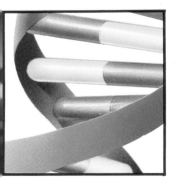
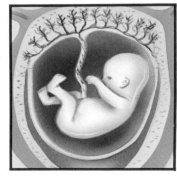
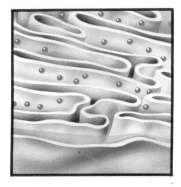
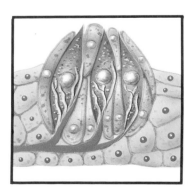

What is your body made of?

Your body is a complex mass of many different parts. All the parts have vital jobs to do and they all have to work properly together to keep you alive and healthy. Your body is made up of more than 50 billion individual living units called cells. All human beings develop from just two cells: an egg cell (ovum*) from their mother and a sperm cell from their father. Egg cells are the largest human cells and can just be seen without a microscope. Most of the other cells can only be seen through very powerful microscopes.**

What is a cell made of?

Although there are differences between the various types of cell, most have the same basic structure and they all need certain substances, such as food and oxygen, to stay alive and to work properly. Here is a cell shown with a section removed so you can see its different parts.

Membrane

This is a fine layer which holds the cell together and separates it from other cells. It is rather like the frontier of a country. It allows certain substances to pass into the cell, while keeping others out. It also allows waste products made in the cell to pass out.

Mitochondria

These are the cell's power stations. Here food and oxygen react together to produce energy so that the cell can live and work.

Ribosomes

Ribosomes are the cell's factories. They manufacture proteins, including those from which the cell itself is made.

Types of cell

You have many different types of cell in your body, each with different jobs to do. (The cells shown here are not to scale.)

◄ Nerve cells have long fibres which send messages to other parts of the body. Some have special endings for feeling sensations.

Muscle cells are long and thin. They can shorten their length (contract) and then relax, which causes movement. ►

Nerve fibre

Tail

Nerve ending

Sperm cells, from the male's body, have long tails. This helps them to swim towards the egg cells in the female's body. ►

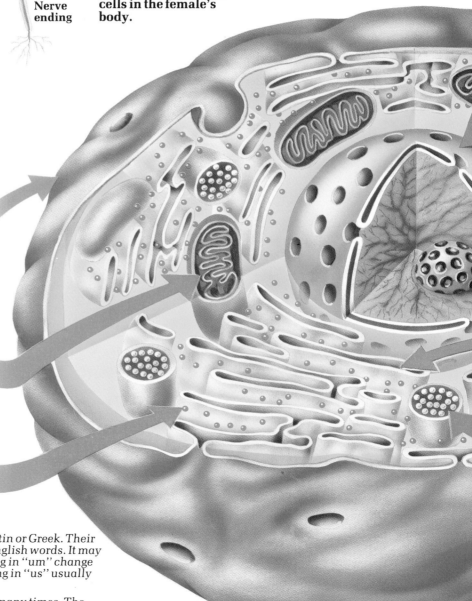

*Many words used to describe the body are Latin or Greek. Their plurals are formed differently from those of English words. It may help to remember that most Latin words ending in "um" change the ending to "a" in the plural and those ending in "us" usually change to "i".

**The cells in this book are shown magnified many times. The colours are not true to life.

Tissues

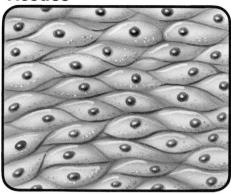

A group of cells of mainly the same type is called a tissue. The minute spaces among the cells are filled with a watery substance called tissue fluid. This picture shows a type of muscle tissue.

Organs

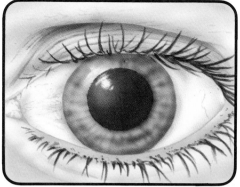

Different types of tissue are grouped together to form organs. An organ has a particular job to do in your body. For instance, your heart pumps blood, your stomach digests food and your eyes enable you to see.

Systems

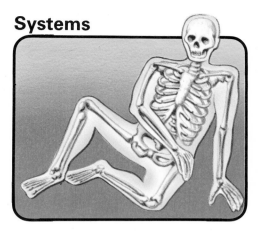

A group of organs whose jobs are closely related is often referred to as a system. Examples are the circulatory system, which includes your heart and blood vessels, and the skeletal system, shown here.

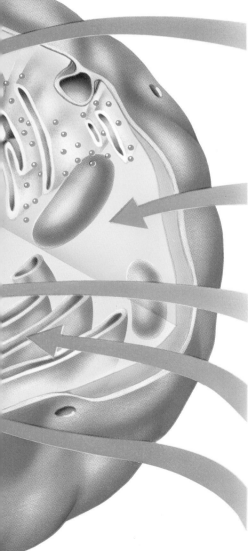

Nucleus

The nucleus acts rather like a government headquarters, controlling and directing all the activities of the cell. It is in the centre of the cell body. (You can see the nucleus in each of the cells on the page opposite.) The nucleus contains special threads called chromosomes. These carry complex coded instructions for the workings of the cell, rather like a computer program. You inherit your chromosomes from your parents.

Cytoplasm

This is a jelly-like substance, which makes up most of the cell, rather like a background landscape. It consists mainly of protein and water, especially water. Your cells are about two-thirds water.

Endoplasmic reticulum

These channels are the cell's industrial estates. They are where the ribosomes are found.

Golgi complex

This acts as a storage depot. Some of the proteins made by the ribosomes are kept here until they are needed.

Lysosomes

These are the cell's secret police. They contain chemicals which destroy harmful foreign substances and any old or diseased parts of the cell.

How cells reproduce

Millions of your cells die every second but new cells are constantly being made to take their place. Some cells live longer than others. The cells lining your intestines get worn away by food and live for only about six days. Red blood cells live for about four months, bone cells for up to 30 years, and nerve and muscle cells, which cannot reproduce, up to a lifetime. A cell reproduces by dividing into two to produce a pair of identical new cells.

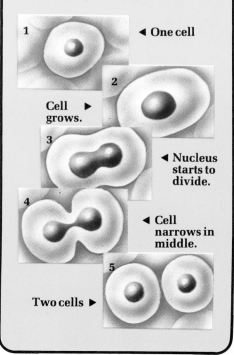

1 ◄ One cell

Cell ► grows.

2 ◄ Nucleus starts to divide.

3

4 ◄ Cell narrows in middle.

Two cells ► 5

Why you eat

Without regular supplies of food to use as fuel your body would soon stop working. Different types of food do different jobs, such as giving you energy or making you grow. To stay healthy you need to eat a good balance of all the types of food described below.

Proteins

Over ten per cent of your body tissue is made of protein so you need to eat protein to renew it and, if you are growing, to make more. The faster you are growing, the more you need. Protein is built up of chemical units called amino acids. Protein in food is broken down in your body into individual amino acids. These are then rebuilt in your cells to form the proteins you need. Good sources of protein are lean meat, fish, cheese, eggs, milk, nuts and beans.

Carbohydrates

These are built up of different sugars (including glucose) and give you most of your energy. You can either eat the sugars directly in foods such as fruit and jam or in the form of starch in foods such as potatoes, rice and bread. Starch becomes sugar inside your body. If you eat more carbohydrates than you need, the excess is converted into a substance called glycogen and stored in your liver and muscles. Or it is converted into fat. It is best to avoid eating sugar in drinks and in foods such as cakes, biscuits, sweets, chocolates and convenience foods. Besides turning to fat, it is bad for your teeth.

Fats

Like carbohydrates, fats provide you with energy. They also form parts of your cells, such as the membranes. Fat is stored in your body and helps to keep you warm. The fats you eat can come either from animals, in foods such as meat, milk, butter and cheese or from plants, in foods such as vegetable oils and nuts. Too much fat may play a part in heart disease.

Vitamins

You need small amounts of about 15 different vitamins so that essential chemical processes can take place in your body. A lack of any particular vitamin causes a specific illness. For example, if children do not have enough vitamin D they get an illness called rickets which stops their bones developing properly.

Minerals

These are involved in vital chemical processes in your body. You need small amounts of about 20 different minerals. Calcium and phosphorus, found in foods such as milk and cheese, help to make your bones and teeth strong. Iron is needed by your red blood cells and is found in foods such as liver and green vegetables. A lack of zinc, found in nuts, fish and fresh vegetables, may cause skin rashes. You also need sodium chloride (salt). In general, people in developed countries eat more salt than necessary. This may be associated with high blood pressure.

Fibre

Fibre, or "roughage", consists mainly of cellulose, which is a type of carbohydrate your body cannot digest. It is found in vegetables, fruit and wholemeal bread. Fibre is valuable because it is bulky and this helps to make the muscles of your intestines (bowels) work efficiently and so prevents constipation. Fibre may help to prevent serious diseases of the intestines, including cancer.

Water

You are losing water all the time in your urine (pee), in your sweat and when you breathe out, so you have to take in water to replace it. There is water not only in drinks but also in solid foods. Lettuce, for example, is nine-tenths water. You could stay alive longer without food than you could without water.

Vitamin	Good sources	Necessary for . . .
A	Milk, butter, eggs, fish oils, fresh green vegetables.	Eyes (especially seeing in the dark), skin.
B (really several vitamins)	Wholemeal bread and rice, yeast, liver, soya beans.	Energy production in all your cells, nerves, skin.
C	Oranges, lemons, blackcurrants, tomatoes, potatoes, fresh green vegetables.	Blood vessels, gums, healing wounds, possibly preventing colds.
D	Fish oils, milk, eggs, butter (and sunlight).	Bones and teeth.
E	Vegetable oils, wholemeal bread and rice, eggs, butter, fresh green vegetables.	Uses not yet understood.
K	Fresh green vegetables, liver.	Clotting blood.

Calories

The amount of energy that can be produced from different foods is measured in kilojoules or Calories*. Some foods have more Calories than others.

650 Calories
250 Calories
80 Calories
50 Calories

The number of calories you need depends on how much energy you use up. Here you can see approximately how many Calories you use doing different activities for an hour. If you regularly eat more Calories than you use up, you get fat. Some people naturally burn up calories faster than others, so they can eat more without getting fat. No one knows exactly why this is.

600 Calories
300 Calories
100 Calories
70 Calories

Getting fat

Fat cells

If you habitually overeat, the excess food is converted into fat and stored in special fat cells. The cells can increase in size and so you put on weight and "get fat". If you eat less than you need, your stores of fat are used up as energy and you get thinner. On average, fat people die younger than thin people. They are more likely to suffer from certain illnesses, including heart disease.

Teeth

There are 32 teeth in a full adult set and 20 in a set of first, or "milk", teeth. Your sharp front teeth, called incisors and canines, are for biting. The back teeth (premolars and molars) have knobbly surfaces for crushing and grinding the food when you chew. There are no premolars in milk teeth and some adults never grow their back four molars (wisdom teeth). Nobody really knows why humans develop two sets of teeth.

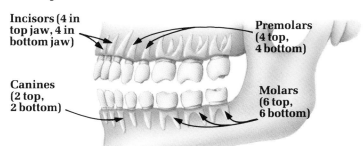

Incisors (4 in top jaw, 4 in bottom jaw)
Canines (2 top, 2 bottom)
Premolars (4 top, 4 bottom)
Molars (6 top, 6 bottom)

What are teeth made of?

Although teeth have different shapes and different jobs to do, they are all built in the same way. Your milk teeth fall out when your adult teeth grow up from underneath and weaken their roots.

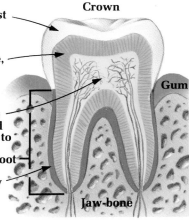

Outer layer of enamel provides a strong biting surface. Enamel is non-living tissue and the hardest substance in your body.

Body of tooth is made of dentine, which is rather like bone.

Soft tissue called pulp contains blood vessels, which supply the tooth with food and oxygen, and nerves, which make it sensitive to pain and temperature.

Root is anchored in jaw-bone by thin layer of bone tissue called cement.

Crown
Gum
Root
Jaw-bone

Tooth decay

Everyone has bacteria (microscopic living creatures) in their mouths. If these get a supply of sugar from sweet foods, they multiply and a substance called plaque is formed. The bacteria produce acids, which eat into the tooth. If the hole is not filled by the dentist, it eventually reaches the pulp cavity and causes toothache. An infection or abscess may develop, or the tooth may become loose if the gum is damaged.

You can help to keep your teeth healthy by eating and drinking less sugary foods, cleaning them properly to remove plaque, using a fluoride toothpaste, which strengthens the enamel, and by going to the dentist for regular check-ups.

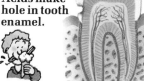

Acids make hole in tooth enamel.

Hole enlarges and reaches pulp cavity.

*1 Calorie = 1,000 calories.

Where food goes to

Before the food you eat can do its job, it has to be absorbed by all the minute cells in your body. First it has to be broken down so that it will dissolve. This process is called digestion and it takes place as the food travels through your digestive tract. The dissolved food then passes into your bloodstream and is carried to all the different parts of your body.

Digestion

Your digestive tract is a long tube which winds from your mouth to your anus (back passage). Most of your digestive organs are in your abdomen. This is separated from your chest by a large sheet of muscle called the diaphragm. Here you can see how food travels through the tract.

1 Your teeth bite and chew the food into small pieces. Saliva (spit), made by your salivary glands, moistens it so it slides down your throat more easily. Saliva contains the first digestive enzyme (see above). This starts digesting starch. (Your salivary glands swell up when you have mumps.)

2 The muscles of your tongue force the food back into your throat (pharynx) and your throat muscles guide it into your gullet (oesophagus). As you swallow, a flap called the epiglottis blocks off the top of the nearby windpipe so the food does not "go down the wrong hole" and make you choke.

Normal position of epiglottis.

Epiglottis covers windpipe when you swallow.

3 The food goes down your oesophagus into your stomach. It does not slide down by gravity but is pushed along by muscles in the oesophagus. This process is called peristalsis and takes place all along your digestive tract. The sound you hear when your "stomach" rumbles is food and air being mixed up and pushed through the tract. In theory, peristalsis means that you could still eat and drink if you were standing on your head.

Tongue

Epiglottis

Salivary gland

Windpipe

Oesophagus

Muscles in oesophagus contract.

Food is pushed along.

Chemical changes are taking place in your body all the time. These are speeded up by enzymes, which are special proteins made in your cells. There are several thousand different sorts of enzyme. Digestive enzymes help to break down and dissolve your food.

How food gets into your blood

The inner wall of the ileum is covered with thousands of tiny structures called villi which stick out like fingers. These give the tube a huge surface area for absorbing the food.

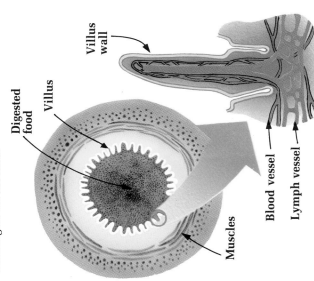

Villus wall

Villus

Digested food

Looking down the tube.

Muscles

Blood vessel

Lymph vessel

The walls of the villi are only one cell thick. The digested food passes through them and into the tiny blood vessels inside. The digested fats do not go directly into the blood vessels. They are absorbed into special "lymph" vessels and enter the blood later.

Being sick

You are sick when your diaphragm muscle and the muscles in the wall of your abdomen contract strongly and force partly digested food back up out of your stomach. It is this stomach juice which makes vomit taste sour. There are many reasons for being sick, including eating too much, eating food that has gone bad and drinking too much alcohol.

Diarrhoea and constipation

Diarrhoea is often caused by an infection in the intestines or by food poisoning. Food travels through the intestines so fast that the water cannot be absorbed properly. If you have diarrhoea, you should drink extra fluid to make up for what you are losing. Constipation is often caused by not eating enough fibre.

Appendix

The appendix has no function in humans, though in animals which eat grass it plays a part in digestion. An inflamed appendix (appendicitis) has to be taken out or it may burst and spread infection right through the abdomen.

Diaphragm

5

4

6

Gall bladder

Large intestine

7

9

Small intestine

8

Appendix

10

Anus

---

4 In your stomach the food is churned about and mixed with stomach juice. This contains enzymes which start digesting protein. It also contains hydrochloric acid, which helps to kill any bacteria swallowed with the food. A meal stays in your stomach for about four hours.

5 Your liver has several important jobs. One of these is to make a green liquid called bile. This acts rather like a detergent. It breaks up the fats you eat into tiny drops so that enzymes can work on them. Bile is stored in your gall bladder.

6 One of the jobs of the pancreas is to make a juice containing many different digestive enzymes. These work on all types of food.

7 The coiled small intestine is only about 4cm in diameter but it is about four metres long. In the first part, called the duodenum, the food is mixed with bile from your liver and with the juice from your pancreas.

8 By the time it gets to the second part of your small intestine (the ileum), most of the food is digested. It passes through the walls of the intestine into your blood. Your blood then carries the digested food to your liver for more processing before taking it round your body.

9 Water and any food which cannot be digested move on into your large intestine. Most of the water passes into your blood through the walls of the first part of the large intestine (the colon). Some of the water passes out of your body later as urine.

10 The more solid waste matter, called faeces, is stored further along your large intestine (in the rectum). The muscles of your rectum push it out through your anus when you go to the toilet.

Why you breathe

Food alone does not give your body the energy it needs. It first has to be combined with oxygen, which is a gas in the air. When you breathe in, oxygen goes into your lungs and from there is carried to all the cells in your body by your blood. Inside the cells the oxygen reacts with glucose (from digested carbohydrates) and the energy stored in the food is gradually released. This process is called respiration. The energy keeps your cells alive and working. During respiration, a waste gas called carbon dioxide, and water, are formed in your cells. You get rid of these when you breathe out.

1 Breathing

Your lungs and windpipe are known as your respiratory system. In this picture the left lung is shown cut open so you can see inside.

When you breathe in, air is sucked through your nose or mouth, down your windpipe (trachea) and into two passages called bronchi. One bronchus goes to the left lung, the other goes to the right. The bronchi gradually divide to form smaller and smaller passages, rather like tree branches.

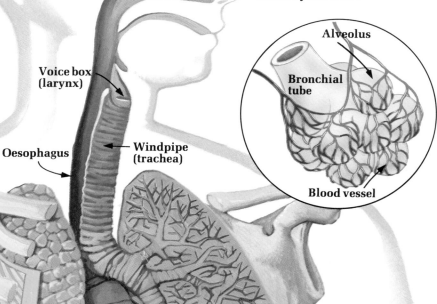

Voice box (larynx)

Oesophagus

Windpipe (trachea)

Rib

Rib muscles

Bronchus

Heart

Diaphragm

2

At the ends of the smallest passages are bunches of air sacs called alveoli. These are like tiny balloons and fill with air when you breathe in. All together there are about 300 million alveoli in your lungs. Their total surface area is about 70 square metres, which is about 40 times the area of your skin.

Alveolus

Bronchial tube

Blood vessel

From body

Alveolus wall

Carbon dioxide

To body

Oxygen

Blood vessel

3

The walls of the alveoli are only one cell thick. The oxygen from the air is able to pass through the walls and into the network of blood vessels which surrounds them. Your red blood cells carry the oxygen round your body. Your blood also carrie[s] back to the alveoli the carbo[n] dioxide produced in your ce[lls] during respiration so that it can be removed from your body when you breathe out.

How cells release energy

Each of your cells contains two special chemicals. One, called ADP, acts like a flat battery. The other, called ATP, acts like a charged battery. When glucose and oxygen pass into the cell's mitochondria (its power stations), they react together, with the help of enzymes. This releases energy, which converts the flat ADP to charged ATP. The ATP then acts as a power supply for the rest of the cell. As its energy is used up, it becomes ADP again and goes back to the mitochondria for recharging.

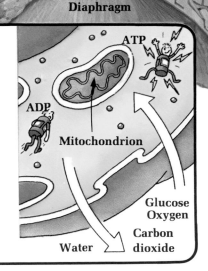

ATP

ADP

Mitochondrion

Glucose Oxygen

Carbon dioxide

Water

1 How you breathe

2

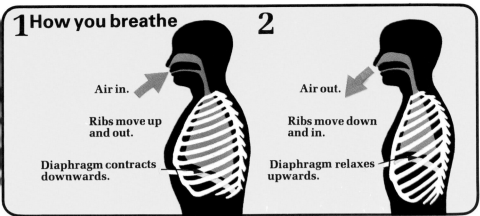

Air in.

Ribs move up and out.

Diaphragm contracts downwards.

Air out.

Ribs move down and in.

Diaphragm relaxes upwards.

Your breathing is controlled by the movements of muscles in your chest, in particular your diaphragm muscle and the muscles between your ribs. To breathe in, your diaphragm contracts downwards while your rib muscles pull your ribs up and out. This expands the space in your lungs, making the air pressure lower inside your lungs than outside your body. Air rushes in to fill the space. When your diaphragm relaxes upwards and your ribs move down and in, the space in your lungs is reduced again and air is squeezed out. Most people usually have about three litres of air in their lungs and exchange only half a litre of it on each breath. During exercise your body needs more energy, so you breathe faster and deeper to take in more air.

Talking

When vocal cords are close together, high-pitched sounds are made.

When vocal cords are open wide, low-pitched sounds are made.

Your voice box (larynx) is at the top of your trachea (see page opposite). When you breathe out, air passes between your "vocal cords". If there is enough air, the cords vibrate and this produces sounds. (These pictures show the vocal cords from above, looking down from the throat.) The muscles of your larynx can alter the shape of the cords. This produces different pitched sounds. By using the muscles of your pharynx (throat), mouth and lips, you form the sounds into words.

Coughing and sneezing

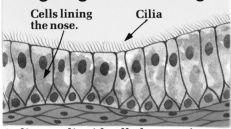

Cells lining the nose.

Cilia

A slippery liquid called mucus is produced in your nose and air passages. This warms and moistens the air you breathe so it can travel along the passages more easily. It also helps to trap dust particles. Tiny hairs called cilia gently waft the mucus away from your lungs towards your nose and throat. If particles irritate your nose, you sneeze them out. If they get into your lower air passages, you cough. When you have a cold, more mucus is produced. This also makes you cough and sneeze, and makes your nose run.

Hiccups

These are caused by your diaphragm contracting more violently than usual so that your in-breaths come in short gasps. The strange noise is caused by your vocal cords suddenly closing. Nobody knows why hiccups start but even unborn babies get them.

Smoking

Late teens

Early forties

Fifties?

Everybody's lungs gradually get blackened by breathing in dirty and polluted air but smokers are particularly likely to develop serious, and often fatal, diseases as a result of inhaling the dangerous chemicals in tobacco smoke. The chemicals irritate the air passages and increase the amount of mucus produced in them. This is one of the causes of "smoker's cough". The chemicals also make the cilia less efficient at clearing the mucus away and so it builds up, making the lungs more prone to infection. Smoking is one of the main causes of bronchitis (inflammation of the air passages) and 90 per cent of lung cancer is caused by smoking. Someone who smokes only five cigarettes a day is eight times more likely to die of lung cancer than a non-smoker. Smoking does not only affect the lungs. The chemicals also get into the blood, reducing its ability to carry oxygen and damaging the heart and blood vessels. Statistics show that if 1,000 children born today all take up smoking, 250 of them will be killed by smoking.

What blood is for

Your blood is your body's transport system. Pumped by your heart, it circulates continuously through all the different parts of your body. Its job is to carry vital substances, such as food and oxygen, to where they are needed and to collect up waste products for disposal. The body of an average-sized adult contains about five litres of blood.

Blood vessels

Your blood travels round your body in tubes called blood vessels. Put end to end, these would stretch for 96,560km, which is more than twice round the Earth. The picture below shows the main blood vessels.

Your blood goes from your heart into your arteries (shown below in red). These have thick, elastic walls because the blood pulses through them at high pressure. The arteries divide over and over again. Eventually they form a network of microscopic vessels called capillaries. These pass between the cells of all the tissues in your body. The capillaries gradually join up together again to form larger vessels called veins (shown here in purple). These carry the blood back to your heart. In your veins the blood flows slower and at lower pressure than in your arteries so their walls are thinner and there are valves to prevent it running backwards. Your heart and blood vessels are known as your circulatory system.

Lung

Heart

Liver

Stomach

Kidneys

Intestines

What is blood?

Blood consists of a mixture of cells floating in a straw-coloured liquid called plasma. Your blood cells are made inside the large bones of your body.

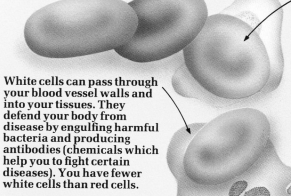

Red cells transport oxygen. As the blood passes through your lungs, oxygen combines with a chemical compound in the red cells called haemoglobin. This changes it to oxy-haemoglobin which is bright red. As the oxygen is deposited in the different parts of your body, the oxy-haemoglobin becomes haemoglobin again and a more purplish red. Red cells have no nucleus.

White cells can pass through your blood vessel walls and into your tissues. They defend your body from disease by engulfing harmful bacteria and producing antibodies (chemicals which help you to fight certain diseases). You have fewer white cells than red cells.

Platelets are tiny fragments of cells. They help to prevent bleeding if a blood vessel is damaged and help your blood to clot when you cut yourself.

Plasma is made up of water, proteins and salts. Digested food substances, such as glucose and amino acids, and waste products, such as carbon dioxide and urea, are transported in the plasma.

In your capillaries

The substances needed by your cells pass out of your blood when it is in your capillaries. The capillary walls are only one cell thick. Plasma and oxygen, from the red cells, are able to pass through the walls and into your tissue fluid. The tissue fluid carries the substances into the individual cells. It also carries waste products from the cells into the capillaries, or else into lymph vessels to be absorbed into the blood later via a vein.

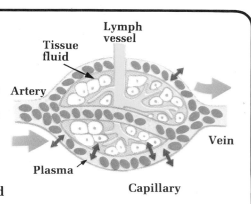

Lymph vessel

Tissue fluid

Artery

Vein

Plasma

Capillary

The heart

Your heart is slightly to the left of the middle of your chest, between your lungs. It is about the size of your fist and is made of muscle. As the muscle contracts, it pumps blood round your body.

The heart is divided into two halves, right and left. Each half has an upper chamber, called an atrium, and a lower chamber, called a ventricle. Your valves open and close as the heart pumps to ensure that the blood does not flow backwards. The beating sound you can hear if you put your ear to someone's chest is made by the valves slamming shut. The first beat is made by the valves between the atria and ventricles, the second by the valves between the ventricles and arteries. Doctors use stethoscopes, which make the beats louder, to help them detect heart abnormalities.

How a valve works

The valve on the right is the sort you have between the ventricles and arteries, and in your veins. Blood flowing in the right direction forces the flaps, or "cusps", open. If it flows in the wrong direction, they are forced shut.

Circulation

Your blood always circulates round your body in the same direction, as shown in this diagram. The whole circuit takes about 45 seconds.

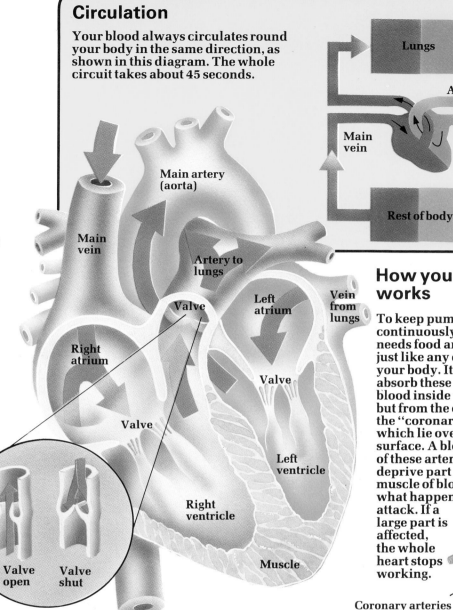

Main artery (aorta)

Main vein

Artery to lungs

Valve

Left atrium

Vein from lungs

Right atrium

Valve

Valve

Left ventricle

Right ventricle

Muscle

Valve open   Valve shut

Lungs

Aorta

Main vein

Heart

Rest of body

How your heart works

To keep pumping continuously, your heart needs food and oxygen, just like any other part of your body. It does not absorb these from the blood inside the chambers but from the capillaries of the "coronary" arteries which lie over its outer surface. A blockage in one of these arteries can deprive part of the heart muscle of blood. This is what happens in a heart attack. If a large part is affected, the whole heart stops working.

Coronary arteries

Pulse

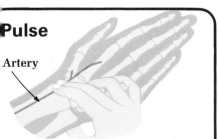

Artery

Every time your heart contracts, your arteries pulsate as blood surges through them. You can feel this at the wrist. The average adult pulse rate is 70 a minute when resting. This increases during exercise because the heart has to pump faster to provide more energy for the muscles.

Heart disease

Heart and circulatory disease is the main cause of death in countries with a high standard of living. The unhealthy lifestyle, which includes overeating, eating the wrong foods, lack of exercise, smoking and stress, makes people more likely to suffer from this type of disease.

Blood groups

Everybody's blood falls into one of four main groups, known as A, B, O and AB. These have different combinations of chemicals called antigens on the surface of the red cells and different antibodies in the plasma. When a blood transfusion is needed, the blood of the donor and patient has to be carefully matched. For example, blood in group A contains "anti-B" antibodies. This means that a person in group A cannot give blood to one in group B or receive blood from them. Mis-matching of blood can cause serious kidney damage to the patient.

About two-thirds of your body consists of water. This has to be kept at a constant level and evenly distributed throughout your cells. You take in water every time you eat and drink, and water is produced inside your cells during respiration. You lose water mainly in your urine, which is produced in varying amounts by your kidneys. In general, the more you drink the more urine your kidneys produce. If you are losing a lot of water, by sweating for example, they produce less. Your kidneys also help to control the level of substances such as salt in your body and they get rid of, or "excrete", waste products such as urea.

Kidneys and bladder

Your kidneys and bladder are known as your urinary system because they produce urine. Your kidneys are at the back of your abdomen, roughly on a level with your waist. The left kidney in this picture is shown cut open so you can see inside.

As your blood passes through your kidneys, any unwanted substances are separated out. This separated fluid, which is urine, passes down two tubes called ureters into your bladder. Your bladder is a muscular bag, which can store up to 400cc of urine. A tight band of muscle, called a sphincter, holds it shut. When you relax the sphincter, the muscles in the walls of your bladder contract and the urine flows into a tube called the urethra and out of your body. The urethra is longer in males than in females because it has to go to the end of the penis.

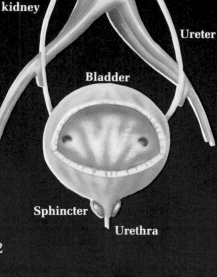

Artery
Vein
Right kidney
Left kidney
Ureter
Bladder
Sphincter
Urethra

Inside your kidneys

Each of your kidneys contains over a million microscopic filtering units called nephrons, like the one shown here. In all, the nephrons filter about 150 litres of fluid a day from your blood though only about 1.5 litres of urine is produced.

1 The blood comes from the artery to this tight knot of capillaries, called a glomerulus, in the nephron.

2 The pressure of blood in the glomerulus forces part of the blood plasma out through the capillary walls and into this cup-shaped structure called a Bowman's capsule. The fluid from the plasma contains water and substances such as glucose, amino acids, salts and urea. (The blood cells, platelets and proteins are too big to pass through the capillary walls.)

3 The fluid goes into this tubule. As it moves along, any of the substances still needed by the body pass out of the tubule and into the network of capillaries surrounding it. These include almost all the water and salts, and all the glucose and amino acids.

4 The reabsorbed fluid goes into a vein and continues circulating round your body.

5 The rest, which consists mainly of water, salts and urea, continues along the tubule and into the ureter, as urine.

What is urea?

Food protein.

Protein broken down into amino acids.

Amino acids rebuilt to form body protein.

Surplus amino acids.

Urea is a waste substance produced in your body. It is made in your liver from any amino acids left over after the protein in your food has been broken down and rebuilt into new protein for your body.

Chemical control

Certain processes in your body are controlled by chemical substances called hormones. These are produced in groups of cells called endocrine glands and are carried all round your body in your blood. Different hormones act on different parts of your body. The picture on the right shows the main endocrine glands.

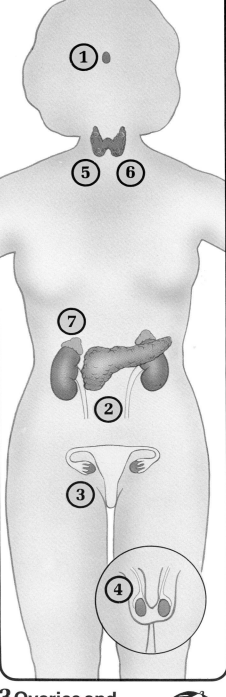

1 Pituitary

This is a pea-sized gland attached to the underside of the brain. It is partly controlled by the brain. The pituitary is sometimes called the master gland because many of its 11 hormones control the actions of other endocrine glands.

Growth hormone is produced by the pituitary. A child with too much may become a giant, one with too little may become a dwarf.

When a baby sucks at its mother's nipple, a hormone called oxytocin is released from the mother's pituitary. It travels to her breast, where it allows the milk to flow.

Antidiuretic hormone (ADH) from the pituitary helps to maintain the correct water balance in your body. It acts on your kidneys and regulates the amount of urine they produce.

2 Pancreas

As well as making digestive enzymes, the pancreas produces the hormone insulin. This regulates the level of glucose in the blood and the conversion of any excess into glycogen. Lack of insulin causes the disease diabetes. This can be treated by insulin injections or tablets.

3 Ovaries and
4 testes*

These glands produce the sex hormones. The female sex hormone, oestrogen, is produced in large amounts in females' ovaries and small amounts in males' testes. The male sex hormone, testosterone, is produced in large amounts in the testes and small amounts in the ovaries. The hormones are not

5 Thyroid

Your thyroid gland is in your neck, at the front of your trachea (windpipe). It uses iodine, which is one of the minerals in food and water, to make two hormones, thyroxine and T_3. These control the rate of respiration in your cells and are essential for the healthy development of new-born babies. If adults have too little thyroid hormone, they become sluggish. If they have too much, they become overactive.

6 Parathyroid

These are four tiny glands buried in the thyroid. They produce parathormone, which helps to regulate the balance of calcium in your blood and bones.

7 Adrenals

Your adrenal glands are just above your kidneys. The outer rim produces several hormones. One of the main ones, called aldosterone, controls the level of salt in your body.

The centre of the adrenals produces adrenaline. When you are afraid or angry, adrenaline pours into your blood and prepares you to take emergency action either by fighting or running away. Your stores of glycogen are converted back into glucose for energy, your breathing rate increases so you get more oxygen, your heart beats faster and your blood is directed towards your muscles.

produced in very large quantities until the age of puberty. This is about 11 in females and 13 in males, though it varies a lot between individuals. At puberty both sexes have a growing spurt and grow pubic hair and hair under the arms. Females' breasts develop, their hips widen, ova are released from the ovaries and menstruation (periods) begins. * Males grow beards, their larynx enlarges and their voice deepens, their shoulders broaden and sperm* are produced.

You can find out more about these on page 27.

Your skin

Your skin is not just a bag to hold your body together. It is an important living organ with several different functions. It protects you from the changing conditions outside your body and from infection. It plays a large part in controlling your body temperature and, by responding to touch, it enables you to sense what is going on around you.* Your skin even plays a part in nutrition because, when it is exposed to sunlight, it makes vitamin D.

Over most of your body your skin is about 2mm thick, though over your eyelids it is only about 0.5mm thick and on the soles of your feet, where it gets a lot of wear, it is about 6mm thick. The skin is arranged in two main layers: the outer epidermis and the inner dermis. This picture shows your skin magnified many times.

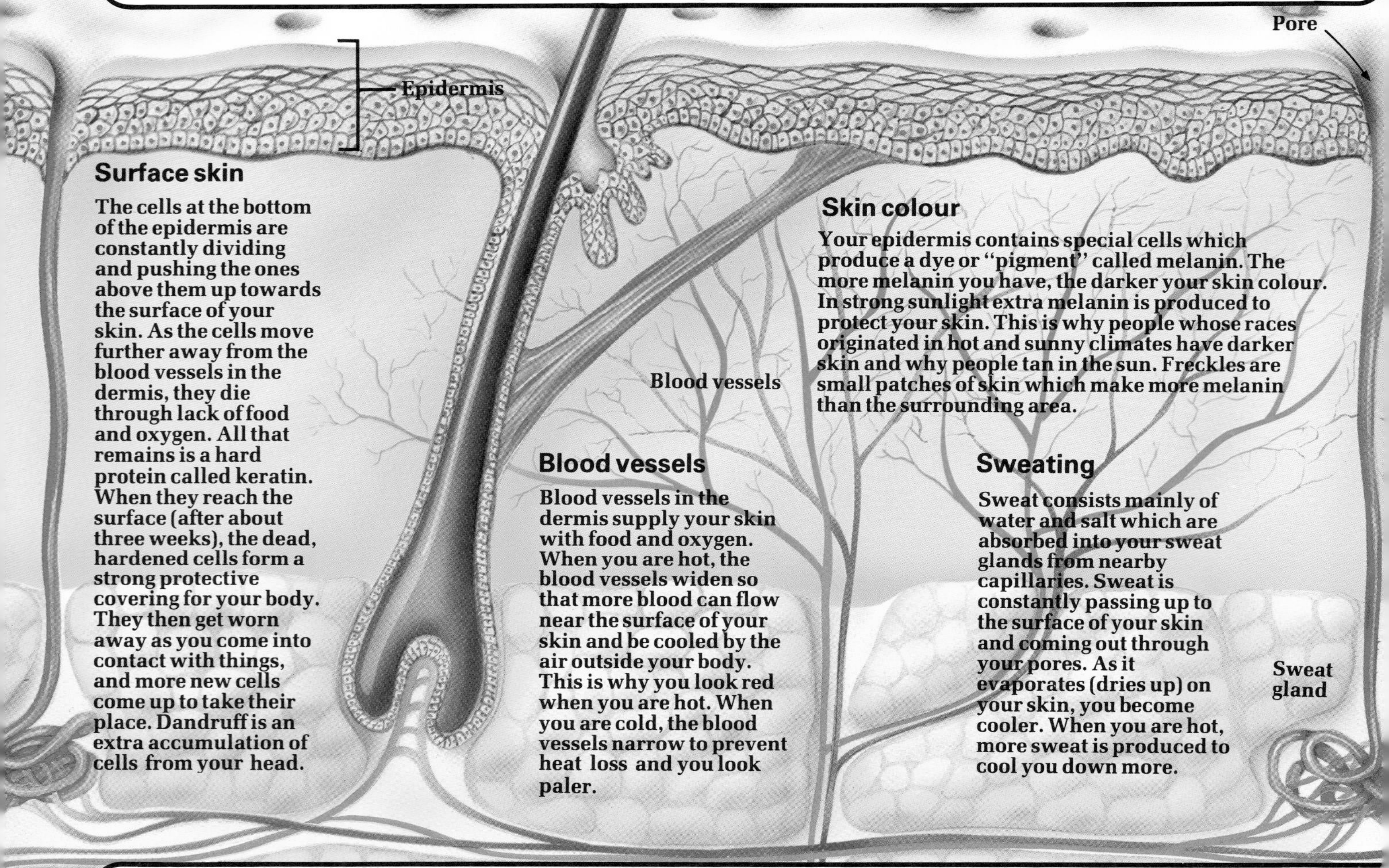

Pore

Epidermis

Surface skin

The cells at the bottom of the epidermis are constantly dividing and pushing the ones above them up towards the surface of your skin. As the cells move further away from the blood vessels in the dermis, they die through lack of food and oxygen. All that remains is a hard protein called keratin. When they reach the surface (after about three weeks), the dead, hardened cells form a strong protective covering for your body. They then get worn away as you come into contact with things, and more new cells come up to take their place. Dandruff is an extra accumulation of cells from your head.

Blood vessels

Blood vessels

Blood vessels in the dermis supply your skin with food and oxygen. When you are hot, the blood vessels widen so that more blood can flow near the surface of your skin and be cooled by the air outside your body. This is why you look red when you are hot. When you are cold, the blood vessels narrow to prevent heat loss and you look paler.

Skin colour

Your epidermis contains special cells which produce a dye or "pigment" called melanin. The more melanin you have, the darker your skin colour. In strong sunlight extra melanin is produced to protect your skin. This is why people whose races originated in hot and sunny climates have darker skin and why people tan in the sun. Freckles are small patches of skin which make more melanin than the surrounding area.

Sweating

Sweat consists mainly of water and salt which are absorbed into your sweat glands from nearby capillaries. Sweat is constantly passing up to the surface of your skin and coming out through your pores. As it evaporates (dries up) on your skin, you become cooler. When you are hot, more sweat is produced to cool you down more.

Sweat gland

Temperature control

Your body is gaining and losing warmth all the time. For instance, you absorb heat from the sun and from hot food and drink. Many of the chemical reactions in your cells, particularly in your liver and muscles, produce heat. You lose heat from any exposed areas of your skin when your body is warmer than your surroundings. Sweating is another way in which you are losing heat continually. Breathing cold air and eating cold food also use up body heat.

These gains and losses have to be balanced so that your body temperature stays stable at approximately 36.5-37°C. When you start to get too hot or too cold, your brain instigates certain changes to stabilize the temperature. These are widening or narrowing of the blood vessels in your skin, more or less sweating, goose pimples and shivering. Shivering works by increasing the activity in your muscles, which helps to produce heat.

Fever

No one really knows why you get a high temperature with certain illnesses. It is as though the brain's "thermostat" is temporarily reset at a higher level than normal. A high temperature is not an illness in itself, only a symptom of illness. The treatment depends on the cause.

* *To find out more about this see page 20.*

Hair

Your hair grows out of pits, known as follicles, in the epidermis. Cells at the root of the hair divide and push it upwards. As it grows further away from the blood supply, it dies and becomes hardened by keratin. Having your hair cut is painless because the hair is dead. About every two years, the cells in the follicle stop dividing and the hair falls out. You are losing hair from your head at the rate of about 50 a day. After a few months rest, the cells start to divide again and a new hair grows. When this does not happen, people eventually go bald. The colour of your hair depends on the amount of melanin in the cells. The shape of the follicles determines whether it is straight, wavy or curly.

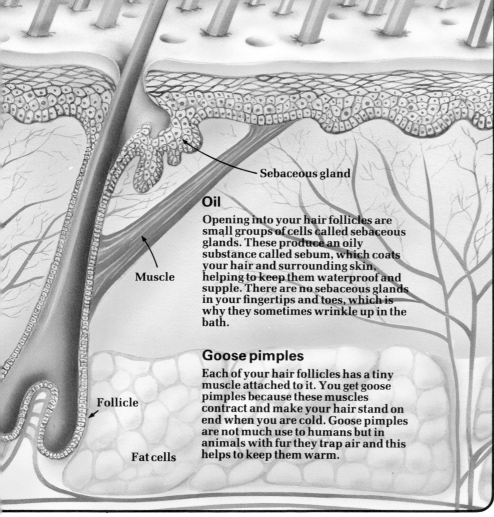

Sebaceous gland

Muscle

Follicle

Fat cells

Oil

Opening into your hair follicles are small groups of cells called sebaceous glands. These produce an oily substance called sebum, which coats your hair and surrounding skin, helping to keep them waterproof and supple. There are no sebaceous glands in your fingertips and toes, which is why they sometimes wrinkle up in the bath.

Goose pimples

Each of your hair follicles has a tiny muscle attached to it. You get goose pimples because these muscles contract and make your hair stand on end when you are cold. Goose pimples are not much use to humans but in animals with fur they trap air and this helps to keep them warm.

Cuts and bruises

When you cut yourself, the platelets and other substances in your blood help it to clot and form a scab. The scab helps to protect the damaged area until new skin grows over it. The new skin grows about 0.5mm a day. When the wound is healed, the scab falls off. A bruise is caused by blood vessels in your skin bleeding into the surrounding tissues.

Spots

Doctors think that spots, or acne, may be caused by changes in hormone levels, especially at puberty. Extra keratin is produced at the openings of the hair follicles and extra sebum in the sebaceous glands, which are most numerous on your face and back. The keratin and sebum accumulate at the openings and form blackheads, or they build up below the surface of your skin causing lumps and pimples. Acne can be improved by special creams from the doctor. Regular washing may help to remove the excess keratin and sebum and sunlight usually helps too. Greasy make-up makes spots worse. Some people find that cutting out foods such as chocolate helps, though there is no scientific evidence for this.

Nails

Nails are the remnants of claws and are formed in a similar way to hair. Each one develops from a row of dividing cells called a root. Your nails grow about 0.1mm a day and the part you can see is made of dead cells hardened by keratin.

Fingerprints

You have hair over almost the whole of your body. The palms of your hands and the soles of your feet are without hair but are covered with tiny ridges instead. This makes them extra sensitive. The patterns made by the ridges on your fingers are your fingerprints. They are formed months before you are born and no two people's are identical.

Information from outside

The information you receive about the outside world comes to you through special nerve cells called receptors. These respond to changes in your surroundings. When they are stimulated by light or sound, for example, they produce tiny pulses of electricity which travel along nerves to your brain. Your brain interprets the impulses and you become aware of what is happening. Many of the receptors are grouped together in sense organs such as your eyes or ears. On the next few pages you can find out how some of these sense organs work.

How you see

The picture on the right shows the inside of an eye viewed from the side, so you can see how it works.

Everything you look at is constantly reflecting rays of light. The rays enter your eyes and fall on the lining at the back of your eye, which is called the retina. Your retina contains receptor cells which are stimulated by the light. They send impulses to your brain, which interprets them so that you see.

1 Every time you blink and your eyelids cover your eyes, tears wash over the surface. The tears keep your eyes moist and help to keep them clean. You blink about 15 times a minute.

2 Your eyelashes help to keep specks of dust and dirt out of your eyes.

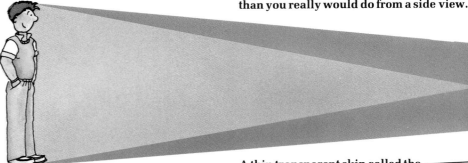

3 The image of the object you are looking at has to be in focus on your retina for you to see it clearly. For this to happen the rays of light have to be bent, or "refracted", when they enter your eye. Light from a near object has to be bent more than light from a distant object. A transparent disc, called the lens, plays an important part in focusing. Its shape is altered by the tiny muscles surrounding it depending on whether you are looking at something near or far away. This makes the light bend the right amount.

4 The image on the retina is upside down because the rays of light cross each other behind the lens.

The black dot in the centre of your eyes is called the pupil. It is really a hole through which the light enters.

The coloured part of your eyes surrounding the pupil is called the iris. It is muscular and alters the size of your pupils. This picture is slightly distorted so you can see more of the iris and pupil than you really would do from a side view.

A thin transparent skin called the conjunctiva covers the front of your eye and helps to protect it.

The proper name for the "whites" of your eyes is the sclera. This is the tough protective outer layer. Round the front of your eye it is called the cornea. The cornea is transparent where it passes behind the conjunctiva.

The centre of your eye, and the part between the cornea and the lens, are filled with clear fluids called humours. These maintain the spherical shape of your eye and play a part in focusing.

Your eyes are set in sockets of bone which help to protect them.

Glasses and contact lenses

These are extra lenses made of glass or plastic which can correct many cases of bad eyesight by helping to focus the image on to the retina.

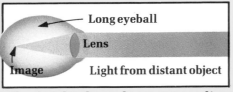

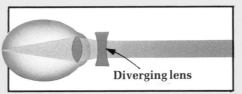

Short-sighted people cannot see distant objects clearly. This is usually because they have long eyeballs and the image of distant objects falls in front of the retina. Short-sightedness can be corrected by wearing lenses which make the rays of light diverge (bend outwards) before they enter the eyes.

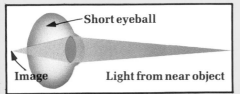

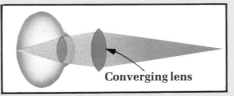

Long-sighted people cannot see near objects clearly. This is usually because they have short eyeballs and the image of near objects falls behind the retina. Long-sightedness can be corrected by wearing lenses which make the rays of light converge (bend inwards) before they enter the eyes.

How rods and cones work

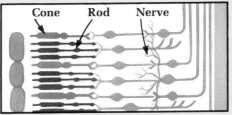

When light falls on the rods and cones in your retina it is absorbed by chemicals contained in them. This changes the structure of the chemicals and triggers off electrical impulses which travel along nerves to your brain. The light-sensitive chemical in rods is known as visual purple or rhodopsin. Vitamin A is used to form it. There are three different types of cone. Each type contains a chemical sensitive to red, blue or green light. All the other colours you see are made up of different combinations and proportions of these three.

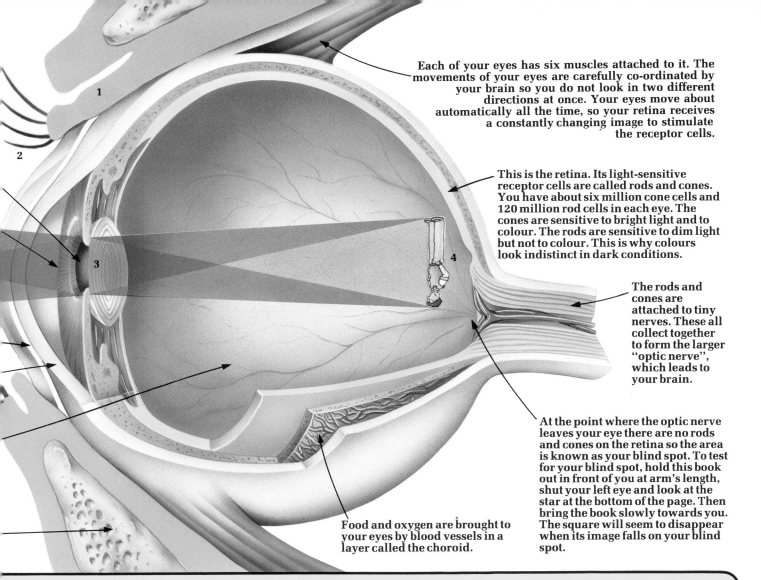

Each of your eyes has six muscles attached to it. The movements of your eyes are carefully co-ordinated by your brain so you do not look in two different directions at once. Your eyes move about automatically all the time, so your retina receives a constantly changing image to stimulate the receptor cells.

This is the retina. Its light-sensitive receptor cells are called rods and cones. You have about six million cone cells and 120 million rod cells in each eye. The cones are sensitive to bright light and to colour. The rods are sensitive to dim light but not to colour. This is why colours look indistinct in dark conditions.

The rods and cones are attached to tiny nerves. These all collect together to form the larger "optic nerve", which leads to your brain.

At the point where the optic nerve leaves your eye there are no rods and cones on the retina so the area is known as your blind spot. To test for your blind spot, hold this book out in front of you at arm's length, shut your left eye and look at the star at the bottom of the page. Then bring the book slowly towards you. The square will seem to disappear when its image falls on your blind spot.

Food and oxygen are brought to your eyes by blood vessels in a layer called the choroid.

Tears

Tears are being produced all the time by your "lacrimal" glands. They drain away into the back of your nose through your tear ducts. When you get something in your eye which irritates it, such as a speck of dust or onion juice, extra tears are produced to wash it away and the ducts overflow. No one knows why human beings cry when they are upset.

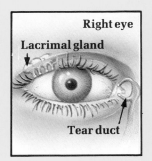

Right eye

Lacrimal gland

Tear duct

Why do you have two eyes?

Having two eyes increases your angle of vision and helps you to judge depth. Try shutting one eye and notice the difference. Although each of your eyes views the same object from a slightly different angle, your brain is able to combine the two separate images on your retinas into one single picture.

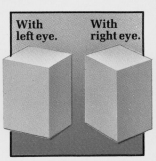

With left eye.

With right eye.

Pupil size

The size of your pupils varies automatically depending on how much light there is. When it is dark, the pupils expand to let in as much light as possible. In bright light they shrink to prevent damage to the retina. Try standing in front of a mirror and shining a torch in your eyes and you will see your pupils shrink.

Colour blindness

Colour blindness affects about eight males in every hundred but less than one female in every two hundred. It is probably caused by faulty cone cells and is usually inherited. Most men who are colour blind find it difficult to distinguish between red and green. Complete colour blindness is very rare.

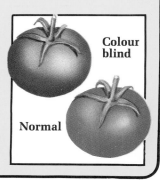

Colour blind

Normal

Hearing

Sound is really vibrations in the air. These stimulate receptor cells inside your ears to send impulses to your brain. Your brain interprets the impulses as sounds. What you can see of your ears is only one part: the outer ear. This leads to your middle and inner ears, which are safely protected within the bones of your skull.

1 The outer ear is more important in many animals than in humans. They can move their ears to "look for" the sounds. Although humans still have the muscles to do this, few people can make them work. Can you?

2 Your outer ear funnels the sounds down this tube, which is called the auditory canal. The canal is lined with hairs and produces wax. Occasionally this builds up and prevents people hearing properly but it can be syringed out safely and painlessly by the doctor.

3 Your outer ear is separated from your middle ear by a tightly stretched membrane called the ear drum. This vibrates when the sounds hit it.
It is not a good idea to poke anything into your ear. Even cotton buds or a handkerchief can damage your ear drum.

4 Your middle ear is filled with air and contains three tiny bones or "ossicles". These are called (from left to right as you look at this picture) the malleus (hammer), incus (anvil) and stapes (stirrup). The stirrup is the smallest bone in your body and is only about 3mm long. Any vibrations of your ear drum pass right along this chain of bones.

8 The impulses travel to your brain along this nerve, called the auditory nerve.

Eustachian tube

5 Your middle ear is separated from your inner ear by another tightly stretched membrane similar to the ear drum. This is called the oval window and vibrates when the stirrup vibrates.

6 Vibrations of the oval window are transmitted to a fluid in the outer channel of this coiled tube. The fluid is called perilymph and the tube is called the cochlea, which means snail. (This is a very simplified picture of the inside of the cochlea.)

7 The vibrations in the perilymph in turn set up vibrations in a second fluid, called endolymph, which fills the inner channel of the cochlea.
The inner channel contains the receptor cells, which have fine hairs attached. Movements in the endolymph pull on the hairs and trigger off electrical impulses in the cells. Some of the hair cells respond only to fast vibrations, which are produced by high-pitched sounds. Others respond only to slower vibrations, which are produced by low-pitched sounds. The louder the sound, the bigger the vibrations and the stronger the impulses produced.

Eustachian tube

The only way air can get into or out of your middle ear is through this tube, which leads to the back of your nose. When you swallow, chew or yawn the entrance to the tube opens and air can pass in or out. This allows the air pressure on both sides of your ear drum to remain equal. The pressure outside your ear sometimes changes suddenly, for example when you are in a lift or aeroplane. The popping sensation you sometimes get then is the pressure equalizing in your middle ear. Swallowing helps to equalize it quicker.

Balance

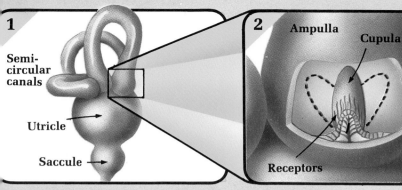

1 Semi-circular canals · Utricle · Saccule

2 Ampulla · Cupula · Receptors

These three semi-circular canals (see opposite page for their position in your ear) and the tiny sacs beneath them, called the utricle and saccule, are filled with endolymph and help you to balance. The sacs tell you what position your head is in and the canals tell you what direction it is moving in.

At the base of each canal is a swollen area called the ampulla. This contains receptor hair cells attached to a jelly-like particle called the cupula. As you move your head, the endolymph in the canals swirls about and pushes the cupula sideways. This pulls on the hairs and triggers off impulses to your brain.

Feeling dizzy

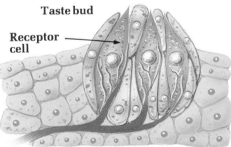

If you spin round and round and then stop, the fluid in your semi-circular canals continues to swirl for a while as though you were still moving. This confuses your brain

because your eyes and muscles are telling it that you have stopped. The result is that you feel dizzy. Travel sickness is also caused by the balance mechanism in your ears.

Why do you have two ears?

Having two ears helps you to tell what direction sounds are coming from. This is because the sound hits one ear a fraction of a second before the other and produces stronger vibrations.

Loud noises

The chart below shows you the approximate loudness of certain sounds. Loudness is measured in decibels (dB). Repeated exposure to loud noise, say through headphones or at discotheques, can damage the receptors in your ears and make you deaf. This type of deafness cannot be helped by wearing a hearing aid.

130dB	Jet aircraft	
110dB	Discotheque	
100dB	Pneumatic drill	
80dB	Heavy traffic	
60dB	Normal conversation	
20 dB	Whisper	

Taste

Taste bud · Receptor cell

Your taste "buds" consist of groups of receptor cells in your tongue which are sensitive to chemicals dissolved in your saliva.

Sour · Bitter · Sour

Sweet and salt · Sweet and salt

Most of the buds are at the sides and back of your tongue. The buds in different areas respond to different tastes. You can only distinguish four basic tastes with your tongue: sweet, sour, salt and bitter. You use your sense of smell to detect more subtle flavours. That is why a lot of food seems to taste the same when you have a cold and your nose is blocked.

Smell

Receptor cells high up at the back of your nose are sensitive to chemicals dissolved in the mucus in your nose. You can smell more when you sniff because this draws air higher up so that more of the chemicals reach the receptors. Human beings can distinguish about 3,000 different smells.

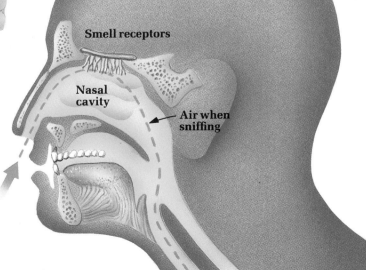

Smell receptors · Nasal cavity · Air when sniffing

Touch

In addition to doing its other jobs, your skin is an important sense organ with many thousands of receptor cells. In general, each receptor responds to only one type of sensation, such as heat, cold, light touch, pressure, pain or itch. This does not mean that all the cells responding to one type of sensation look the same. Here is a selection of receptor cells.

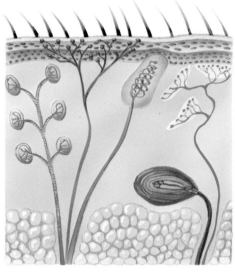

In the skin of some areas, such as your lips, fingers and the soles of your feet, you have many more receptors than elsewhere. Here you can see how the male human body might look if it was proportioned according to the sensitivity of its different parts. You can see why it is that even a tiny stone in your shoe often feels enormous and why it is sometimes difficult to find the exact spot of an itch in an area like your back.

The communications network

The information received by your senses has to be sent to your brain so your brain can sort it out and give your body instructions how to respond. The instructions as well as the information are transmitted in the form of electrical impulses along your nerves. Your nerves, together with your brain and spinal cord, make up your nervous system. Your spinal cord is a continuation of your brain which runs down your spine (backbone).

The nervous system

This is a simplified picture of the nervous system showing how nerves reach to all parts of your body. Each nerve (shown here in orange) consists of a bundle of nerve fibres. Each fibre is part of a nerve cell, or "neurone". Most of the cell bodies are in your brain or spinal cord, which are known as your central nervous system. Some of the fibres are very long, for example those stretching from your spinal cord to your feet.

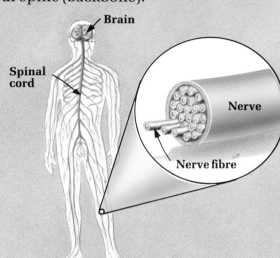

Brain

Spinal cord

Nerve

Nerve fibre

How nerves work

You have about 100 billion neurones in your body. There are three main types. Sensory neurones, which is a term sometimes used for receptor cells, carry impulses from your sense organs to your central nervous system. Motor neurones carry impulses back from your central nervous system to your muscles and glands. Connector neurones within the central nervous system pass the impulses from one cell to the next. The simplest types of responses you make to information provided by your senses are automatic ones, called reflex actions. Pulling your hand away from a prickly thistle is a reflex action. Below you can see how it comes about.

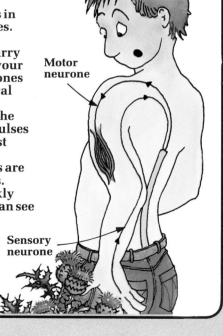

Motor neurone

Sensory neurone

1
Pain receptor in your hand, which is at end of a sensory neurone, is stimulated by thistle.

2
Electrical impulses travel along nerve fibre.

3
Nerve fibres are insulated by a sheath made of a fatty substance called myelin.

What is an impulse?

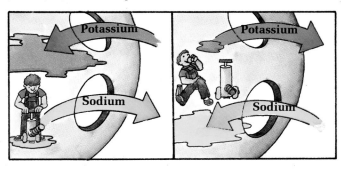

The electrical impulses in your body are caused by changes in the balance of the minerals sodium and potassium in your cells. Normally you have a lot of potassium inside your cells but not much sodium. This is because your cell membrane is constantly pumping sodium out into the surrounding tissue fluid. Outside the cells there is a lot of sodium and not much potassium. An impulse is produced by a momentary change in the cell membrane which allows sodium to pass into the cell and potassium to pass out. The impulse travels along your nerves at a speed of 120 metres per second. After it has passed, the normal chemical balance is restored by the sodium pump.

How impulses pass from one cell to another

Impulses cannot jump the tiny gaps between one cell and the next but are passed across chemically. The branches at the end of nerve fibres finish in "terminal buttons". These contain many energy-producing mitochondria, and pockets, called vesicles, which contain a chemical "transmitter". When an impulse reaches the buttons, the transmitter is released. It crosses the gap, which is called a synapse, to the dendrites of the next cell body and when enough has accumulated an impulse starts in this neurone.

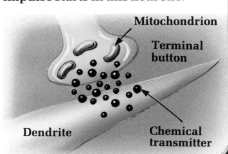

Mitochondrion

Terminal button

Dendrite

Chemical transmitter

Test your reflexes

Doctors use this test to see whether people's reflexes are working properly. Sit with your legs loosely crossed and ask someone to tap sharply just below your kneecap with the side of their hand. When they hit the right spot, your leg will jerk upwards. This is a reflex action.

Funny bone

Close to your funny bone, at your elbow, is a nerve which is less well protected than most. When you bang the bone you can feel an impulse shoot down your arm and make it tingle.

Autonomic nervous system

This is a secondary system of nerves. Although you are usually unaware of it, a series of automatic responses is taking place all the time in this system to control processes such as digestion, breathing and circulation. Many of the cell bodies of the neurones in the autonomic system are outside your brain and spinal cord in small groups called ganglia. The ganglia receive information from receptor cells in the various organs of your body and then send out appropriate instructions to muscles, such as your heart, and glands, such as your salivary glands. The system is self-regulating and helps to keep your body in a balanced state.

10 Branching end of motor neurone is embedded in the muscles of your arm. When impulses reach the muscles, they contract and pull your hand away from the thistle.

9 Impulses pass out of central nervous system along fibre of motor neurone.

8 Impulses pass across branching end of connector neurone to dendrites of the motor cell body.

7 Connector neurone passes impulses on.

6 The body of the next cell, a connector neurone, has these branches called dendrites. They pick up impulses from the sensory neurone.

5 Neurone has a branching end.

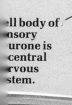

ll body of nsory urone is central rvous stem.

The human computer

The human brain is a bit like a computer. Your senses provide the input, your brain processes all the information, and the instructions sent to your muscles and glands are the output. The nerves throughout your body are like wires. The network of interconnecting neurones in your brain is far more complex and versatile, however, than the circuits of any computer, even though a computer can handle larger quantities of information. No computer can do anything until it has first been programmed by a human brain. The pictures on the right will give you an idea of how some of the different areas in your brain work. Very little is known about many other areas. They are probably to do with thinking, memory and decision-making.

Parts of the brain

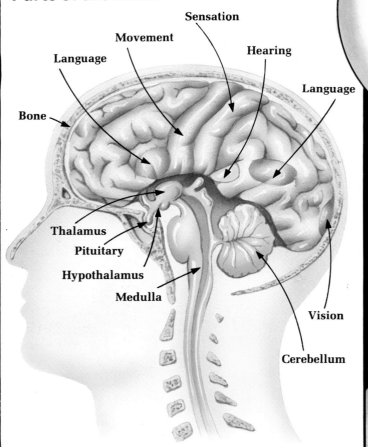

Language
Movement
Sensation
Hearing
Language
Bone
Language
Thalamus
Pituitary
Hypothalamus
Medulla
Vision
Cerebellum

A section of the brain in this picture has been removed so you can see where some of the areas described on the right are positioned. Your brain is protected by the bones of your skull and by a thin layer of fluid which acts as a cushion around it. Your brain has a large number of blood vessels. The brain cells are active all the time, even when you are asleep, so they need a continual supply of food (in the form of glucose) and oxygen. If the cells are without oxygen for more than about four minutes, they are permanently damaged.

Movement

Conscious movements are controlled by the "motor" area. Motor neurones send impulses from here to the muscles in different parts of your body. The more precise the muscle movements, the more of the motor area involved. On the "map" of your body in the area, your hands and mouth take up the most space. The map is upside down because your feet are controlled by cells at the top of your brain and your face by cells lower down.

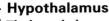

Language

Special language areas understand and process what you read or hear. They also send impulses to the nearby motor areas of the mouth and larynx in preparation for speech.

Smell

The smelling area interprets impulses from your nose with help from your memory.

Hypothalamus

The hypothalamus has several different jobs. It forms part of your autonomic nervous system and helps to keep conditions in your body constant. It regulates hunger and thirst, and body temperature. It also controls the release of many of the hormones from your pituitary gland (see page 13). Emotions, such as fear, anger and excitement, and also sex drive, are partly determined by the hypothalamus.

Pituitary

Thalamus

You feel pain in a part of your brain called the thalamus. Impulses then travel on to the sensation area so that you can tell where the pain is coming from. Pain helps to protect you by warning you of danger both from outside and inside your body. It often causes an automatic reflex action even before you are aware of the sensation.

Medulla

The medulla regulates essential functions such as heart rate and breathing and continues to work even when you are asleep. It also controls swallowing, coughing, sneezing and vomiting. Like the hypothalamus, the medulla is part of your autonomic nervous system.

Sensation

This area receives impulses from the receptors in your skin. As in the motor area, your whole body is mapped out in the brain cells, so that you can be aware of the exact spot of each sensation. The most sensitive parts of your body (see page 20) have the most space in your brain. The cells which appreciate taste are also in this area.

Hearing

The hearing area receives impulses from the cochlea in your ears. It can tell how loud a sound is from the strength of the impulses and what pitch it is by which cells in the cochlea are sending them. To tell which direction the sound is coming from, it compares the strength and timing of the impulses from each ear (see page 19).

Vision

Impulses from your retina travel to the vision area. Here the cells respond to particular simple patterns such as a straight line or a corner. Your brain then builds the patterns up into more complex images, probably by comparing and combining them with information in your memory stores.

Memory

Memories are stored in your brain in at least two stages, one for recent memories and one for more long-term ones. Nobody really knows how memory works. Initial short-term memory probably comes about because impulses travel round the brain cells repeatedly along certain pathways. For long-term memory and learning, a permanent change must take place in the chemical make-up of the cells or in the pathways.

Cerebellum

The cerebellum helps you to balance and co-ordinate your movements. It receives impulses from parts of the body such as your ears, eyes and muscles, integrates all the information and then adjusts the action of your muscles so your movements are smooth and accurate.

Two halves of the brain

The large, folded part of your brain is in two halves, which are known as the left and right cerebral hemispheres. Both hemispheres have corresponding areas for dealing with information from your senses and with movement. The nerves from the two sides of your body cross each other as they enter your brain, so that the left hemisphere is associated with the right side of your body and the right hemisphere with the left side.

Each hemisphere also has specialized areas. In right-handed people the left hemisphere controls the use of language and numbers, while the right hemisphere specializes in recognizing objects (including faces) by their shape and probably in appreciating music. In most left-handed people it is the other way round. 91 per cent of people are right-handed.

Sleep

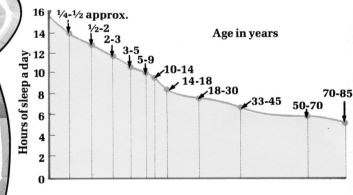

There are two kinds of sleep. One is known as active or rapid-eye-movement (REM) sleep, because your eyes move around even though they are closed. The other is known as quiet or non-REM sleep. Altogether you spend about 20 per cent of each night in active sleep and it is during active sleep that you dream. The activity in your brain can be measured by a machine called an electroencephalogram (EEG), which produces a pattern of waves. The waves produced during active sleep and when you are awake are similar. The reason for sleep and dreams is not really understood. In quiet sleep your muscles relax, and your heart and breathing rates fall, so this may be a period of recovery and repair for your body. Active sleep may be an important part of learning. The diagram above shows how people sleep less as they get older.

How you move

You are able to move because of the way your nervous system, muscles and bones all interact. Your nervous system sends impulses to your muscles, which are attached to your bones. The impulses make the muscles contract (shorten), this pulls on the bones and you move.

What is bone made of?

Only 30 per cent of your bones consists of living tissue. The rest is non-living tissue, mainly minerals. This is what makes the bones hard.

The inner part of the bone is arranged in a meshwork, which makes it both strong and light. It is sometimes called spongy bone.

Bone has a thin, tough outer layer called the periosteum. If you break a bone, cells in the periosteum multiply and grow over the break, joining the two parts of the bone together again.

Many of your large bones contain a soft tissue called red marrow. Your red blood cells (5 billion a day) and your white blood cells are made in the marrow. Some bones also have yellow marrow, which contains fat cells.

This is a strong layer of compact bone. The living bone cells are arranged in rings around central canals containing blood vessels and nerves. Calcium and phosphorus are deposited by your blood among the cells. As well as making the bones hard, these minerals are needed for many of the chemical reactions in your body. Your bones act as a storage depot for them. Also among the cells are fibres of a protein called collagen. These help to make the bones resilient.

Skeleton and muscles

On the right you can see the bones of the right side of your body and the muscles of the left side. Many of your muscles are arranged in layers over your skeleton. You have over 200 bones. As well as allowing you to move, they give your body a strong framework and help to protect your internal organs. For example, your rib cage protects your heart and lungs. You have over 600 muscles. Like your bones, they all have names. The buttock muscle, which is the largest, is called the gluteus maximus.

Cranium (skull)

Clavicle (collar-bone)

Scapula (shoulder-blade)

Sternum (breastbone)

Rib cage

Humerus

Vertebrae (backbone)

Radius

Ulna

Pelvis (hip-bone)

Femur

Coccyx (remnants of a tail)

Patella (kneecap)

Tibia

Fibula

1 Joints

The place where two bones meet is called a joint. Some joints, those of the bones in your skull for example, are fixed but most are moveable. There are several different types of moveable joint. Here are just three of them.

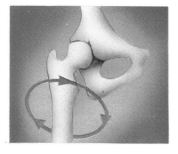

Ball and socket joints, at your hips and shoulders, move in all directions.

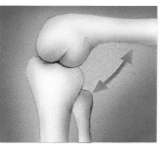

Hinge joints, at your knees and elbows, move in two directions only, like a door opening and shutting.

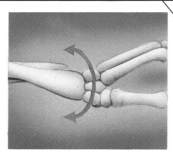

Pivot joints, at your wrists, twist so that you can turn your hands over.

How muscles work

The type of muscle that covers your skeleton is known as striped muscle because that is how it looks under a microscope. The type in organs such as your bladder, and in your digestive tract and blood vessels, is known as smooth muscle. Smooth muscle is controlled by your autonomic nervous system. Below you can see how striped muscle works.

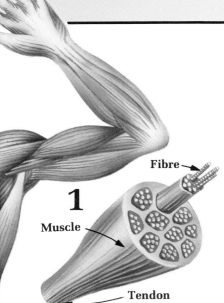

Fibre

Muscle

Tendon

1 A muscle consists of bundles of long thin cells, often referred to as muscle fibres. The muscle and each of the bundles are enclosed in sheaths of the protein collagen. At each end of the muscle the sheaths join together to form a strong, flexible "tendon".

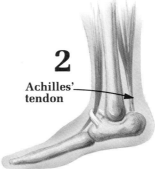

Achilles' tendon

2 Tendons join your muscles to your bones. You can see and feel the largest tendon in your body (the Achilles' tendon) just above your heel. You can also see tendons on the inside of your wrist when you clench your fist and at the inside of your elbow when you bend your arm.

3 Each muscle fibre has a motor nerve ending embedded in it and each fibre contains interlocking strands of two different proteins: actin and myosin. When an impulse reaches a fibre, a chemical transmitter is released. This releases energy in the cells' mitochondria and makes the strands of actin and myosin move closer together, so that the muscle becomes shorter (contracted) and fatter.

4

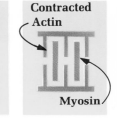

Motor nerve ending

Relaxed

Contracted
Actin

Myosin

5 The contracting muscle pulls on the bone to which it is attached and makes it move. The force of the movement depends on how many of the fibres contract at once. If you point your toe as hard as you can, your calf muscle will bulge out. This is because all its fibres are contracted. If you point your toe only slightly it will bulge less because fewer fibres are involved.

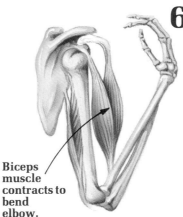

Biceps muscle contracts to bend elbow.

6 Most of your muscles are arranged in opposing pairs. For instance, as your biceps muscle contracts to bend your elbow, your "triceps" relaxes to allow the movement. When you want to straighten your arm again, the triceps contracts and the biceps relaxes. Special stretch receptors in your muscles let your brain know what your body is doing without your having to look at it.

Triceps contracts.

2

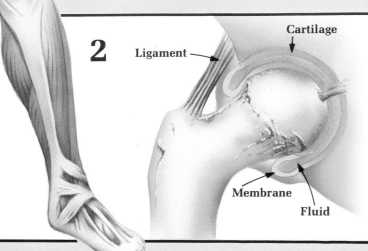

Ligament

Cartilage

Membrane

Fluid

The ends of the bones at a moveable joint are cushioned by pads of a smooth, rubbery protein called cartilage. (Your ear lobes and the squashy bit at the end of your nose are also made of a type of cartilage.) The joint is surrounded by a thin, slippery membrane. This produces a fluid which lubricates the joint. Without cartilage and fluid, your bones would grind against each other when you moved. The bones are held together by strong, flexible collagen fibres called ligaments. If a ligament is forced beyond its limit, it may tear. This is a sprain. If the bones slip out of place they are said to be dislocated. Someone who is described as being double-jointed does not really have two lots of joints, they just have extra-long ligaments.

Why exercise?

Exercise is an important part of keeping healthy. Without it muscles waste and are replaced by fat, joints stiffen up, and breathing and circulation become less efficient. There is an increased risk of becoming overweight and of developing certain illnesses, especially heart disease. Exercise alone is not enough to get the body really fit. It has to be combined with other aspects of a healthy lifestyle, such as eating a balanced diet and not overeating, smoking or drinking much alcohol.

How to get fit

Stamina, suppleness and strength are all different aspects of fitness. As you can see from the chart below, different sports vary as to which of these they develop. For example, yoga is excellent for suppleness and weightlifting for strength. The best all-round exercise is swimming. To get the benefit of any type of exercise you have to do it regularly. Be careful to build up the amount you do gradually as you get fitter. There is no point in getting completely exhausted, or in doing a sport you don't like. An important benefit of enjoyable exercise is that it helps you to relax and overcome stress, which can cause illness.

A = Stamina. B = Suppleness. C= Strength.

Sport	A	B	C
Badminton	✷	✷✷	✷
Cycling	✷✷	✷	✷✷
Dancing (energetic)	✷✷	✷✷✷	✷
Football	✷✷	✷✷	✷✷
Gymnastics	✷	✷✷✷	✷✷
Ice skating	✷✷	✷✷	✷✷
Hill walking	✷✷✷	✷	✷✷
Horse riding	O	O	✷
Jogging	✷✷✷	✷	✷✷
Judo	✷✷	✷✷✷	✷✷
Roller skating	✷✷	O	✷
Skipping	✷✷	O	✷
Squash	✷✷	✷✷	✷
Swimming	✷✷✷	✷✷✷	✷✷✷
Tennis	✷✷	✷✷	✷
Walking	✷	O	O
Weightlifting	O	O	✷✷✷
Yoga	O	✷✷✷	O

O – no effect. ✷ – beneficial effect. ✷✷ – very good. ✷✷✷ – excellent.

Stamina

Stamina, or endurance, is the ability to keep doing something for a period of time without it becoming a strain. Even walking up a flight of stairs can be a strain for an unfit person and make their heart beat a lot faster than usual. In very simple terms, the fitter you are, the more exercise you can do without your heart rate rising substantially and the better you feel in general.

Muscle tone

Even when you are still, your muscles are not completely relaxed. Some of the fibres have to be contracted just to keep you sitting up. This slight state of tension is known as muscle tone. When people talk about "toning up", they mean firming and strengthening their muscles by exercise.

What is aerobics?

Aerobics means "with air". Aerobic exercise increases your ability to get oxygen round your body. To be aerobic, a sport has to be strenuous but not exhausting and you have to keep it up steadily and continuously (for at least 12 minutes at a time). Sports such as swimming, jogging and cycling can all be aerobic. Ones like sprinting and squash are not because they require short bursts of energy. These sports are anaerobic.

During aerobic exercise, your body makes a steady demand for more oxygen and you breathe deeply and more fully. Your heart works harder and over a period of time this strengthens it and makes it more efficient. Your circulation improves, with your blood vessels becoming more elastic and new channels opening up. All this increases your stamina and helps to reduce your risk of developing heart disease.

Getting tired

During aerobic exercise your muscles get a lot of their energy from the glucose in your bloodstream. During intense exertion your heart and lungs cannot get glucose and oxygen round your body fast enough so your muscles convert their own glycogen stores without oxygen (anaerobically). At the same time a substance called lactic acid is produced. As this builds up, your muscles start to tire and ache. This is one reason you cannot keep the exercise up for long.

Sex and babies

A baby develops when a female's ovum (egg cell) and a male's sperm cell meet and join together in a woman's body after a man and woman have had sex (sexual intercourse). The moment when the ovum and sperm join is called fertilization or conception. Together the two cells make one new cell. This grows and develops into a baby in the woman's womb. Both the male and female reproductive systems start working fully at puberty (see page 13).

1

1 Most of the female sex organs are in the lower part of the abdomen, between the bladder and the rectum.

2 The ovum is drawn into this tube, called an oviduct or Fallopian tube, by the fringed end. This is where fertilization usually takes place.

3 The egg passes into the womb (uterus). This is a hollow organ with thick muscular walls and many blood vessels. Its lining changes in response to changes in the levels of female hormones. Every month, from puberty to the menopause, it thickens in preparation for a fertilized ovum to embed itself in it. If the ovum is not fertilized, the lining disintegrates and the woman has a period (menstruates). The lining passes out of the vagina along with blood.

1 The ova are stored in the ovaries from birth. Every month, from puberty to the age of about 45, an ovum matures in one of the ovaries and is released. This is called ovulation. The time when ovulation stops is called the menopause.

4 The vagina is a stretchy tube leading from the uterus to the outside of the body. Glands in the lining produce a lubricating mucus.

5 Outside the female's body is the vulva. This consists of two folds of skin called labia (lips) which cover (from back to front) the opening of the vagina, the opening of the urethra (the tube from the bladder) and a sensitive mound of tissue called the clitoris.

2

1 Most of the male's reproductive organs are outside the abdomen. Inside it would be too warm for sperm production to be very efficient.

2 Two tubes, called sperm ducts, carry the sperm to the penis. The ducts open into the urethra. The sphincter muscle at the opening of the bladder prevents urine from passing down the urethra at the same time as sperm.

3 Two glands (the prostate and Cowper's) produce fluids which the sperm swim in. Semen is the mixture of sperm and the fluids.

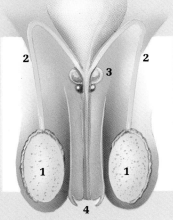

1 From puberty, sperm are produced in tiny tubes inside the testes. The sperm are stored in a coiled tube called the epididymis, which lies over the back of the testes.

4 The penis contains soft, spongy tissue and many blood vessels. The most sensitive part, at the tip, is called the glans. It is partly covered by a loose fold of skin called the foreskin.

3

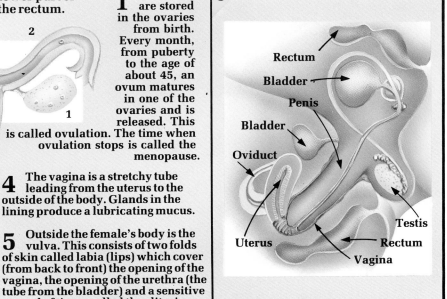

Rectum
Bladder
Penis
Bladder
Oviduct
Uterus
Testis
Rectum
Vagina

During sexual excitement the penis gets larger and stiff (erect) because it becomes congested with blood. The glands in the vagina increase their production of lubricating mucus. During intercourse, the penis fits inside the vagina. At the climax of intercourse (orgasm), muscles around the male's urethra contract, squirting (ejaculating) semen into the female's vagina and muscles in the female's vagina and uterus contract rhythmically. The sperm swim up through the uterus and into the oviducts. One ejaculation contains about 300 million sperm but only about 100 get as far as the oviducts before they die. If there is an ovum in one of the oviducts, fertilization may take place.

Contraception

There are several ways of preventing an ovum and a sperm joining and causing pregnancy. Some are more effective than others. After each method of contraception described below there is a percentage figure. This shows how many women in a hundred get pregnant using that method for a year. Without contraception, 80 per cent get pregnant.

THE PILL. These contain hormones, usually oestrogen and progesterone. They prevent ovulation and are prescribed by a doctor. (Almost 0%)

IUCD (Intrauterine contraceptive device). This is a small piece of plastic or metal which is inserted in the uterus by a doctor. It works partly by preventing an ovum from settling in the uterus. (2%)

CAP OR DIAPHRAGM. This is a thin, cap-shaped piece of rubber which the woman puts in her vagina, over the entrance to the uterus, before intercourse. To be safe, it has to be used with a spermicide (a cream which makes sperm inactive). (3% when used carefully)

CONDOM OR SHEATH (Johnny or rubber in slang). This is a thin rubber sheath which is put on to the erect penis to catch the semen. For extra safety the woman uses a spermicide. (3% when used carefully)

1

A baby starts to develop as soon as the ovum and sperm have joined together to form one new cell. First the cell divides to form two identical cells. These two cells then divide to make four, the four divide to make eight, and so on, until a solid ball of dividing cells is formed.

One sperm enters ovum (fertilization).

Ovum

Cell divides.

Ball of cells.

2

The ball embeds itself in the thickened lining of the uterus. As the cells continue to divide, they gradually become different from one another and start to develop into different tissues and organs. At this stage the future baby is called an embryo. After a month, when it is only about 5mm long, its developing heart is already beating. The embryo is contained in a protective bag of fluid called the amniotic sac.

3

After two months, all the main parts of the body are formed, though not yet fully developed. The embryo is about 3cm long and weighs about 1g.

While a baby is in the uterus, it gets its food and oxygen from a special organ called the placenta. This develops partly from the mother's tissues, partly from the embryo's, and contains blood vessels from each of them. The food and oxygen pass from the mother's blood vessels into the baby's across a thin separating membrane. They get into the baby's body through a vein in its "umbilical cord". Waste products from the baby's body pass out through two arteries in the cord and into the mother's blood. When a baby is born it is still attached to the placenta by the cord. Your navel (tummy button) is the remains of your umbilical cord.

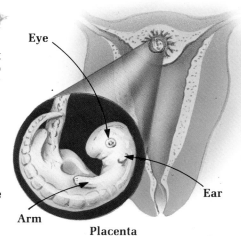

Eye

Ear

Arm

Placenta

Umbilical cord

Amniotic sac

Taking after your parents

A baby develops in the way it does because of two sets of "instructions", one in the ovum and one in the sperm. These instructions are in the chromosomes of the cells (see page 3). The ovum and sperm have 23 chromosomes each, making a total of 46 when they join together at fertilization. An exact copy of these 46 chromosomes is passed to every cell in the baby's body and stays with it for life. Because it has one set of instructions from each parent, it takes after both of them.

Chromosomes are made of a chemical called DNA (deoxyribonucleic acid). This looks rather like a twisted ladder. The rungs of the ladder consist of two pairs of small chemicals called adenine and thiamine, and guanine and cytosine. The order of the rungs varies and forms a code. A sequence of about 250 rungs gives the instruction for one particular characteristic, such as an enzyme, a hormone or a blood group. Each of these coded instructions is called a gene. There are hundreds of genes on each chromosome.

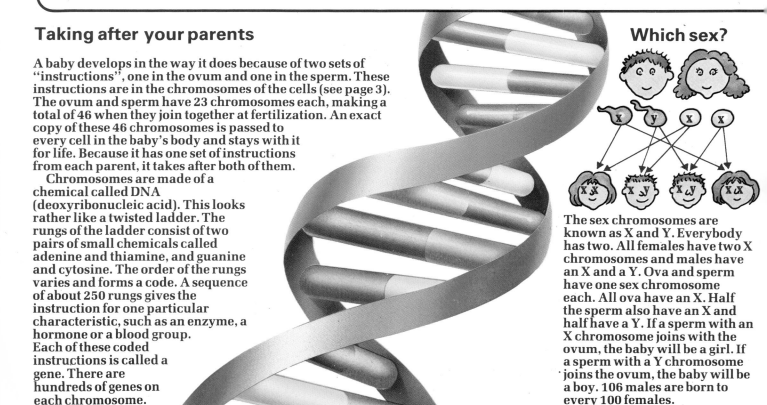

Which sex?

The sex chromosomes are known as X and Y. Everybody has two. All females have two X chromosomes and males have an X and a Y. Ova and sperm have one sex chromosome each. All ova have an X. Half the sperm also have an X and half have a Y. If a sperm with an X chromosome joins with the ovum, the baby will be a girl. If a sperm with a Y chromosome joins the ovum, the baby will be a boy. 106 males are born to every 100 females.

4

The baby continues to develop for another seven months. As it grows, the mother's uterus enlarges from its normal length of about 8cm and volume of about 3cm^3 to a volume of about 6,000 cm^3 (6 litres). The baby starts to move about and kick. It also sleeps, can hear loud noises and even suck its thumb.

5

Sometime during the last few months most babies settle into a head-down position in the uterus.

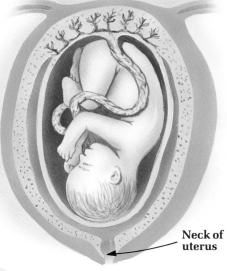

Neck of uterus

6

Most babies are born about 40 weeks after the date of the mother's last period. The process of giving birth is called labour. During the first stage, the muscles of the uterus start to contract, at first quite gently, then more and more strongly and frequently. This forces the baby downwards, so that its head stretches the neck of the uterus. This is the hardest part of labour and usually lasts about 12 hours. The amniotic sac usually bursts during this stage and the fluid flows out of the vagina.

The second stage is when the baby's head eventually starts to pass through the neck of the uterus. The mother helps by "pushing" and the baby passes into the vagina, which expands, and out of the body. This stage usually lasts about half an hour. Most new-born babies are about 50cm long and weigh about 3kg.

Finally, more contractions of the uterus force the placenta (now called afterbirth) out through the vagina.

Hair colour

Most of your characteristics, your height and intelligence for example, are determined by many different genes and also by the conditions you grow up in. A few characteristics, such as the colour of your hair, are determined chiefly by one gene from each of your parents. The genes of the parents above could be combined to produce three different hair colours in their children. A dark hair gene is said to be "dominant" because it overrules genes for other hair colours. A fair hair gene is dominant over a red hair gene. To have red hair, you have to inherit a red hair gene from both your parents. Eye colour works in the same way. Brown is dominant over blue.

Twins

One birth in about 80 produces twins. There are two sorts. Non-identical, or "fraternal", twins are produced when two ova happen to be released at the same time and both are joined by separate sperm. These twins have different chromosomes, so they are not necessarily alike and can be of different sexes.

Identical twins are produced when the ball of dividing cells splits into two at a very early stage and each part goes on to develop into a separate baby. These twins are identical and always the same sex because they have identical chromosomes.

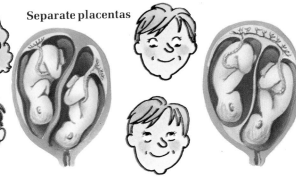

Twins usually have separate placentas.

Separate placentas

Shared placenta

Things that go wrong

There are many reasons for things going wrong in the human body. Here you can find out about some common types of diseases and ways of fighting them. The things you feel when you are ill, such as a headache or a pain in the abdomen, are the "symptoms" of your illness.

Congenital diseases

These are diseases that people are born with. They are often caused by faulty chromosomes. Babies who have Down's syndrome, for example, have 47 chromosomes in their cells instead of 46. This may make them physically or mentally handicapped.

Accidents and injuries

Most accidents happen in the home, on the roads and, to a lesser extent, in industry. The old and the very young are especially prone to accidents, the old to falls, for example, and babies to suffocation.

Cancers

These are the third most common cause of death in countries with a high standard of living, after accidents and heart and circulatory disease. A cancer is a disorder of cell growth. In normal tissues the cells divide and multiply only under carefully regulated conditions. A cancer cell (also called a malignant cell) is one that has undergone a change which frees it from this regulation. It divides and multiplies without control, damaging healthy cells in the process. As well as growing in one place to form a tumour (swelling), malignant cells can spread around the body and start up other tumours. (Not all tumours are cancerous. Some are fairly harmless.)

Cancers usually develop in older people though anyone may be affected. They can start in any part of the body. Some parts most commonly affected are the lungs, breasts, colon, skin and blood (this is called leukaemia).

TREATMENT. New discoveries are being made about cancer all the time and many people with the disease can now be cured. There are three main types of cancer treatment. Some tumours can be removed in an operation, some are damaged by radiation (radiotherapy), and some can be destroyed by very strong drugs (chemotherapy).

Degenerative diseases

These are caused by the body tissues gradually wearing out, or "degenerating", with use and old age. Loss of sight, deafness and arthritis (inflammation of the joints) can all be degenerative diseases.

Heart and circulatory disease

The formation of a blood clot in a blood vessel is called a thrombosis. This is one of the most common causes of a heart attack (see page 11). If the thrombosis is in one of the arteries to the brain, part of the brain is deprived of blood and is damaged. This is a "stroke". The symptoms, paralysis or loss of speech for example, depend on which area is affected.

BLOOD PRESSURE. This is the force with which blood is pumped through the arteries. (It is not the same as pulse, which is the rate at which it is pumped.)

People with persistently high blood pressure have an increased risk of heart attacks or strokes. Low blood pressure sometimes causes fainting when not enough blood reaches the brain. Fainting is a reflex action. When you fall over, gravity brings the blood back to your brain. It can also be caused by blood collecting in your legs when you stand still for too long.

Mental illness

There can be many reasons for mental illness. Stress from the environment is often part of the cause. Examples of mental illnesses are severe depression and anorexia nervosa (when young women stop eating properly because they are obsessed with being thin).

Environmental diseases

These are caused by harmful substances in the surroundings. The lung disease asbestosis, for example, is caused by asbestos dust. One of the dangerous chemicals in exhaust fumes is lead, which may interfere with the development of children's brains. Radiation, from nuclear bomb tests, for example, may cause cancers. It can also damage chromosomes and so harm future generations.

Infectious diseases

Most of these are caused by microbes, or micro-organisms, which are living things so small they can only be seen with a microscope. Not all microbes cause disease. Many are living in or on your body all the time quite harmlessly. Some are even used to make foods such as cheese, yoghurt and bread.

VIRUSES. These are the smallest microbes. They can only grow inside living cells. They invade your cells and use the cells' resources to multiply. This damages the cells and produces the symptoms of disease.

Many illnesses are viral. A serious one is polio; milder ones include colds, influenza (flu), measles, chicken pox, mumps, German measles, cold sores from herpes (type 1) and verrucae (a type of wart on the sole of the foot).

BACTERIA. These are single cell microbes, about 0.001mm long. They reproduce by dividing, sometimes very rapidly. A disease may be caused either by the harmful bacteria themselves damaging your tissues or by poisons (toxins) which they produce.

Bacterial diseases include TB (tuberculosis), typhoid, pneumonia, whooping cough, tonsillitis, tetanus, boils and some kinds of food poisoning.

HOW INFECTIOUS DISEASES SPREAD. Many infectious diseases spread through the air. An infectious person breathes, sneezes or coughs out microbes and another person breathes them in. Colds, flu and measles are spread in this way.

You can also get infections from food or water. Diseases such as typhoid and food poisoning are transmitted like this. Two ways food can be infected are by people and flies.

Many skin diseases, such as boils and warts, are transmitted by touch. Diseases spread in this way are called contagious diseases.

STD (SEXUALLY TRANSMITTED DISEASE). This is a group of contagious diseases which are also known as VD (venereal disease). They are caught by having sexual intercourse with an infected person. The microbes which cause the illnesses die quickly away from the warmth and moisture of the body so you cannot catch them from toilet seats, dirty sheets or towels. Gonorrhoea (known as clap) and herpes (type 2) are well known STDs. Most STDs can usually be cured if they are treated early. No cure has yet been found for AIDS. This is caused by a virus known as HIV which is transmitted in semen and blood. Many large hospitals have special STD clinics which give confidential advice and treatment.

The body's defences

Your body has several natural defences against disease. One of the most important is your white blood cells. Some of these engulf and destroy harmful bacteria, while others produce antibodies which fight various foreign invaders.

Some of the white cells which produce antibodies are formed in your lymph vessels, in lymph glands. When you have an infection more white cells are formed than usual, to help you fight the disease. This sometimes makes the glands swell up and you can feel them in your neck, armpits and groin.

Once your white blood cells have been stimulated to produce an antibody against a particular disease, they can produce it again very quickly if necessary. This is why you rarely get illnesses such as measles more than once. After the first attack, you become "immune".

Immunization

This is a way of making your body immune without it having to suffer the disease. The virus, bacteria or toxins which cause the illness are specially treated so they become harmless. They are then injected into you (or in the case of polio are swallowed). This makes your body produce antibodies against the disease and you are protected from it in the future.

Sometimes antibodies themselves are injected when there is no time for the body to learn to produce its own, during an epidemic for example.

Allergies

Some people develop antibodies to normally harmless substances such as pollen, feathers and food. The antibodies act against the person's own tissues and produce the symptoms of allergy.

Transplants

Many operations can now be performed to transplant tissues or organs (heart, kidneys, cornea) from one person to another. The main problem with transplants is that the white blood cells of the patient regard the foreign tissue as dangerous and produce antibodies to destroy it. Drugs can be used against the white blood cells but this then leaves the patient with very little resistance to infection. To help prevent tissue rejection donors are chosen with tissues as similar as possible to the patient's.

Drugs

Drugs are chemicals you can take to alter the way your body works. Many, such as aspirin, relieve symptoms; others, such as anti-cancer drugs, can cure disease. An important group of drugs is antibiotics, including penicillin. These can kill or stop the growth of many of the bacteria which cause infectious diseases.

EVERYDAY DRUGS. Coffee, tea and cola drinks all contain stimulants (drugs which speed up your body processes). Nicotine, in tobacco, is a drug which acts on the nervous system. (See page 9 for more about smoking.) Alcohol also affects the nervous system, including the brain. People who drink a lot of alcohol can become physically as well as psychologically dependent on it.

All drugs, including these everyday ones, can cross the placenta in pregnant women and harm the developing baby in various ways.

DRUG ABUSE. This is when drugs are taken in ways and doses not intended by doctors. Drugs which act on the nervous system to alter mood are the ones most commonly abused. People who take them frequently may become both psychologically and physically dependent. There is a danger of overdose and of serious long-term side effects. The main types are strong pain killers, such as heroin, morphine and cocaine; sedatives (sleeping drugs) including barbiturates and diazepam (valium); and stimulants including amphetamines and LSD (acid).

Glue sniffing has an effect similar to alcohol. Dangers include unconsciousness, vomiting and choking, with possible long-term damage to the kidneys and nervous system.

Cannabis (also called pot, hash, grass, marijuana) also makes you feel "high". Its long-term side effects are not yet known.

Kidney machines

People with kidney failure can use kidney machines to filter their blood. The blood is fed down a tube from one of the patient's blood vessels and into the machine. It passes alongside a bath of special "dialysis" fluid. The waste, and excess water and salts, pass into the fluid and the clean blood is returned to the patient's blood vessel. This takes many hours and has to be done several times a week. A strict diet also has to be followed.

Looking inside the body

There are various ways a doctor can see inside a person's body and so diagnose illnesses more easily.

X-RAYS. These are a type of electromagnetic ray which can pass through body tissues. If X-rays are directed at the body and a photographic plate is placed behind it, an image is produced on the plate. The X-rays pass through soft tissues easily and these show up black. They are partly stopped by bones, which show up white.

ULTRASOUND SCANNERS. Ultra high frequency (UHF) sound waves are bounced off the different organs. The waves make a pattern, which is displayed on a screen and can be interpreted by the doctor. This is a useful way of examining babies in the uterus because it is harmless.

CAT (COMPUTERIZED AXIAL TOMOGRAPHIC SCANNERS). X-rays are directed at the body from several different angles at once. A computer helps to interpret the images produced and a "slice" through the body is shown on a screen.

MAGNETIC SCANNERS. These are just being developed. An electromagnet makes the body produce radio waves and a computer builds up an image from them.

Index

First published in 1983 by Usborne Publishing Ltd, Usborne House, 83-85 Saffron Hill, London, EC1N 8RT. Copyright © 1991, 1983 Usborne Publishing

The name Usborne and the device ♉ are Trade Marks of Usborne Publishing Ltd. All rights reserved.

Printed in Italy